D1100050

This Little Hippo
book belongs to

_____

_____

Scholastic Children's Books,
Commonwealth House, 1-19 New Oxford Street,
London WC1A 1NU, UK
a division of Scholastic Ltd

London ~ New York ~ Toronto ~ Sydney ~ Auckland

First published by Scholastic Ltd, 1998

Developed from the original book The Night After Christmas,
by James Stephenson. The Forgotten Toys is an animated series produced
by Hibbert Ralph Entertainment for Link Entertainment,
scripted by Mark Holloway,
directed by Graham Ralph and produced by Karen Davidsen.
Executive producers: David Hamilton and Claire Derry.
Script adaptation by Norman Redfern. Book illustrations by Maureen Galvani and Les Gibbard.
All rights reserved.

2 4 6 8 10 9 7 5 3 1

ISBN 0 590 19967 6

Printed in Belgium

The Forgotten Toys

Toys on Trial

Little Hippo

Teddy and his friend Annie, the ragdoll, were lost. Somewhere, a little boy and his sister were waiting for them to come home. But which way was home?

Late one night, as the rain poured down, they stopped outside a jeweller's shop. Behind the railings there was a doorway where they could shelter for the night. Annie slipped between the railings and waited for Teddy to follow, but he was too plump to squeeze through.

"Come on!" said Annie, pulling him by the paw.
Teddy tumbled through on to the floor and found himself behind bars.

"It's like being in prison," he complained.

"Sssh!" hissed Annie, ducking into the shadows. "Someone's coming!"

Keef and Kath were notorious burglars. They tiptoed up to the railings and looked all around. The coast was clear. Keef took a hammer and chisel out of his bag and smashed open the railings. A bell began ringing above their heads. It was the burglar alarm!

Teddy was still sitting on the floor. Keef grabbed him and stuffed him in between the bell and its hammer. The bell stopped ringing, and the two burglars dashed into the jeweller's shop.

"Are you all right?" Annie asked Teddy.

"No-o-o-o!" juddered Teddy.

"I'll find something to get you down," promised Annie.
She crept into the shop and found a broom. Kath was watching
Keef push a stick of dynamite into the door of the safe.

"After we've pinched the jewels, we'll split up and meet at the
pub," Keef told Kath. "The 'Sprout and Sausage', got it? Split up,
'Sprout and Sausage'."

"Sprout up, split and sausage," replied Kath.

Keef lit the fuse, then he and Kath dived for cover. There was an enormous explosion, and smoke filled the shop. Jewellery flew all over the place. When Annie opened her eyes, she saw a beautiful diamond ring on the floor. She picked it up, grabbed the broom, and rushed out to help Teddy.

"What ha-a-a-ppened?" Teddy shuddered.

"I was blown up!" said Annie.

She aimed the broom at Teddy and gave an almighty shove. Teddy shot out of the top of the burglar alarm and flew through the air.

Meanwhile, Keef and Kath were escaping. Kath had all the jewels in a sack on her back, and as she dashed out of the shop, Teddy fell into it!

"Help!" shouted Teddy. "Pigtails!"

"Oh, no!" cried Annie. "Teddy!"

But he was already too far away to hear her.

Annie was still sitting sadly near the shop doorway when the police arrived with their dog, Skip.

"Are you a burglar, Miss?" Skip asked Annie. He wasn't a very clever dog.

"No, but I saw them," said Annie. "They stole my friend, Teddy."

"Then I must ask you to accompany me to the Station," said Skip. "Come along, please."

The Chief of Police wasn't happy. He took Annie's photograph, and he took her fingerprints, too. But how could a doll help him solve the crime?

"You saw it all," he told her. "You know where they've taken Lady Muster's priceless diamond cluster! If only you could talk!" Annie didn't say a word. The Chief turned on his heels and stormed out of his office.

Meanwhile Kath was trying to remember where she had to meet Keef.

"'Spit and Polish'," she muttered, "'Spot and Drawbridge' . . . 'Trout and Sandwich'?"

"'Sprout and Sausage'!" piped a voice from inside the sack.

"Who said that?" squeaked Kath in surprise.

Back at the Police Station, Annie sneaked out of the Chief's office. She pushed the heavy door, squeezed through, and ran straight into Skip.

"Where do you think you're going?" the dog asked her.

"The burglars have taken Teddy," Annie explained. "If you help me rescue him, I'll help you arrest the burglars!"

"I can't," sighed Skip. "The Chief has just sacked me because I have never managed to arrest anyone."

"Help me catch the robbers," insisted Annie, "and they'll give you your job back."

Annie didn't wait any longer. There was an alarm button on the Police Station wall. She pushed it. The Chief of Police rushed out, spotted Skip, and sprang into action.

"He's got the doll!" he shouted. "After him!"

"Let's go, Skip," said Annie. "To the Sprout and Sausage!"

The Chief of Police was pedalling his rusty bicycle as fast as he could, but he still couldn't catch Skip and Annie.

"We've lost him, Miss," grinned Skip.

"But we need him to come with us to catch the burglars!" Annie pointed out.

"I forgot that," said Skip. "I'd better slow down!"

Keef and Kath had already met up at the 'Sprout and Sausage'. Keef tipped the sackful of loot on to a table. Out tumbled Teddy.

"What's this?" asked Keef.

"It's a teddy bear, Keef," replied Kath.

"Never mind that," Keef snapped, throwing Teddy on to the floor. "Where's Lady Muster's diamond cluster?"

"I don't know, Keef," said Kath.

"It's in that bear, isn't it?" Keef said. "You've hidden the ring inside that teddy!"

He reached down to grab Teddy, but Teddy wasn't there. Knowing he was in great danger, he had crawled under the pool table. He was safe, but not for long.

"There he is!" shouted Keef. "Put him on the pool table. I'm going to open him up!"
Kath placed Teddy on the pool table.

"She's hidden Lady Muster's diamond cluster inside you somewhere," said Keef, menacingly, "and there's only one way to get it out!"

He picked up a spoon from the bar, and stood over Teddy with a horrible smile on his face.

Suddenly, the door flew open, and Skip and Annie raced in.

"It's them!" cried Annie. "Catch them, Skip!"

Skip bounded across the room and chased Keef and Kath into a corner. Teddy jumped off the pool table, grabbed the bag of jewels, and handed it to Skip. The Chief of Police burst into the room.

"Come here, Skip!" he shouted. "Bad dog! I'm sorry, but that dog's barking mad!"

Keef and Kath couldn't believe their luck.

"That's all right," smiled Keef. "We were just leaving, weren't we, Kath?"

"That's right," nodded Kath. "Don't forget the bag, Keef."

Keef tried to grab the bag from Skip but the police dog shook his head, and the jewels spilled out all over the floor.

"You're the burglars!" said the Chief.

"She is, not me," said Keef.

"No, it's him," argued Kath.

"Well, I'm arresting you both," said the Chief. "Now, where's Lady Muster's diamond cluster?"

"He's got it!" cried Kath.

"No, she's got," shouted Keef.

While the burglars were arguing, Skip wandered sadly outside.
Annie followed him.

"Skip," said Annie, "what's wrong?"

"He's not going to give me my job back," sighed Skip.

"But you caught the burglars," said Annie. "And you found
the jewels."

"But we didn't find the diamond cluster," said Skip.

"I did," Annie grinned. "I took it to stop the burglars stealing it."

The Chief handcuffed the burglars, and was trying to search them, when Skip ran in, barking excitedly.

"That's enough from you," the Chief began. Then he noticed the diamond cluster. "You've found it! Well done! You must have your job back at once – and a promotion!"

Teddy, Annie and Skip watched the Chief lead the burglars away.

"Thank you, Miss," said Skip.

"Thank you for helping us," replied Annie. "Goodbye, Sergeant Skip!"

The Police dog scampered off happily in search of unsolved crimes and fiendish villains. Annie and Teddy walked away down the street. They were searching, too. But their search would only end when they found their way home.